THE AWFUL ORPHAN ELF

GILLIAN JOHNSON

Hodder
Children's
Books

A division of Hachette Children's Books

First published in Great Britain in 2013
by Hodder Children's Books

I

A Catalogue record for this book is available
from the British Library

ISBN: 978 1 444 90358 4

Typeset and designed by Fiona Webb

Printed and bound in Great Britain by
CPI Group (UK) Ltd, Croydon, CR0 4YY

Hodder Children's Books
a division of Hachette Children's Books
338 Euston Road, London NW1 3BH
An Hachette UK company
www.hachette.co.uk

For Thomas and Nicholas

It was a warm spring day at

MONSTER HOSPITAL and with
no monsters in their Emergency Department
the doctors went outside to play.

Carolyn untangled her skipping rope, Sylvie put on her flippers to swim laps in the moat,

Tom lolled in the grass to read a book,
and Dylan practised headers.

When looking up they saw ...

CHOP-CHOP-CHOP.

The helicopter landed on a mound of moss and an ugly little leprechaun tumbled out.

Is this Monster Hospital?

'It is,' said Carolyn. 'My Alfonse needs a doctor!' he said. 'Where are the doctors?'

'**We** are the doctors,' said Sylvie.
'You *can't* be doctors. **You're just ... kids!**'

Carolyn, Sylvie, Tom and Dylan frowned.
Kids, yes. But by now they were also
experienced doctors who understood
monsters and their medical problems –
or most of them anyway.

'Do you want us to help or not?' asked Sylvie.

The leprechaun pulled out a piece of paper. 'Alfonse has hurt his head,' he said. 'As soon as he wakes up, I need one of you to sign this Release Form.'

'Maybe we should **admit** him before we **release** him,' said Tom.

'Good point,' said the leprechaun. 'You guys are smarter than I thought.'

'Two of us are girls,' snapped Sylvie.

'Did you say a head injury?' said Tom.

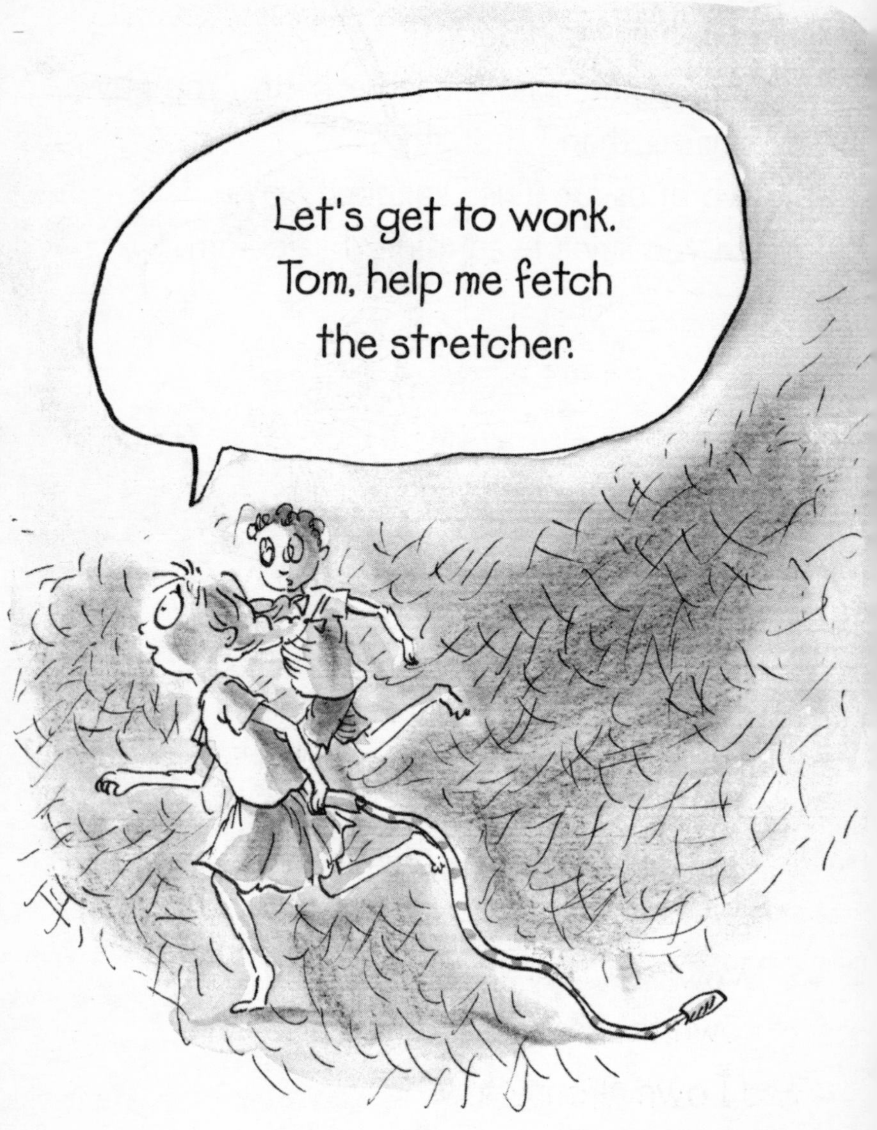
Let's get to work. Tom, help me fetch the stretcher.

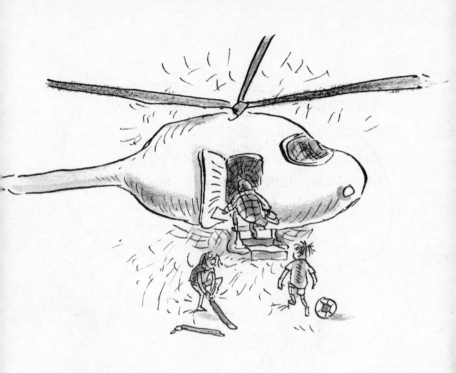

'Dylan and I will stabilize the patient,' Sylvie said, kicking off her flippers. 'What is he?' she asked the leprechaun.

'Footballer!' he replied. 'Star of Orphans United.'

'Wow!' said Dylan.

'I own the team,' said the leprechaun.

'And I own Alfonse too.'

'I *meant*,' said Sylvie, 'what kind of
monster is Alfonse?'

'He's an elf,' said the leprechaun.

Inside the helicopter, they found the patient
bundled up on the seats.

Alfonse was quite small but strong-looking with waxy orange skin.

'Are you his father?' asked Sylvie.

'Yes,' the leprechaun replied slowly.

'But you're a leprechaun and he's an elf,' Sylvie pointed out.

'With one eye!' Dylan crowed.

'I adopted him,' the leprechaun mumbled.

Sylvie checked the patient's pulse. 'A bit rapid,' she said.

'A real, live, one-eyed footballer!' Dylan was excited.

'He won't be **live** for long if we don't treat him,' muttered Sylvie.

'How long has he been unconscious?'
asked Dylan.

'Twelve hours,' said the leprechaun. 'He got
hit on the head during a game, but didn't pass
out till later. I couldn't wake him last night –
or this morning.'

'When he was awake did he have a headache?' asked Sylvie.

'Yes.'

'Vomiting?'

'He threw up on the pitch.'

'Pain in the neck or back?'

'I dunno,' said the leprechaun. 'I just need you to fix him up so he can play tomorrow.'

'We'll really try,' said Dylan.

Sylvie glared at Dylan. 'He won't be kicking a football tomorrow,' she said, 'if he's in a coma today.'

'But it's the final game!' cried the leprechaun.

'That's too bad,' said Sylvie. 'Head injuries are very serious, Mr ...'

'Leonard.'

'Mr Leonard, how exactly did Alfonse hurt his head?'

Carolyn and Tom arrived with the stretcher
and lab coats for Sylvie and Dylan and the
four doctors loaded the patient.

'Careful. He may have a cervical fracture,'
said Tom.

'What's that?' asked Dylan.

'Broken neck,' said Tom.

They carried the patient out of the helicopter ...

... and into the X-ray room of the hospital.

'The Monster Body Scan (MBS) machine is the best way to find out what might be going on with Alfonse's brain,' Sylvie told Mr Leonard. 'I'm afraid you will have to wait outside.'

They positioned Alfonse and
pressed the button.

The machine whirred and buzzed and finally spat out a series of images.

The doctors gathered to discuss their findings.

'There is no structural damage to the brain or spinal cord,' Sylvie began. 'There is no fluid in his brain sac. And though his pupil is small, his reflexes are normal.'

'So what's going on?' said Dylan.

'If he was not asleep,' Tom suggested,

'I would say he has a straightforward concussion and would just require observation for 7–10 days.'

Dylan leapt up.

'We need to take a full medical history when he wakes,' said Sylvie. 'Find out if this is Alfonse's first concussion.'

'But why?' asked Dylan.

'Two or more concussions put a monster athlete at *serious* risk of permanent damage!' said Tom.

'If Alfonse has had a concussion before, he needs to quit football for at least six months,' said Sylvie.

'Brains are more important than football games,' said Sylvie.

'You going to tell that to Mr Leonard?' asked Carolyn.

'Yes, and you're going to help me!' said Sylvie.

'But ...'

'Let's go and check on Alfonse,' muttered Tom, rushing off with Carolyn.

Dylan and Sylvie found Mr Leonard pacing the waiting room. 'I want one of you to sign this,' he said.

'I'm not signing anything,' said Sylvie. 'But we do need to know more about Alfonse's injury.'

'Yes, tell us about the troll who sat on his head,' said Dylan.

Mr Leonard was annoyed. 'Alfonse is a striker. Amazing speed. As he was running, about to score, the captain tripped him. Then he sat on his head. He got a red card but the damage was done.'

'So you took Alfonse out of the game?'

'No. He took the penalty kick!'

'**What?**' gasped Sylvie.
'You let him play with a head injury?'

'He wasn't at his best,' admitted Mr Leonard. 'But Alfonse not on best form is still better than the rest. He scored two more goals and only came off when he threw up. They don't like vomit on the pitch.'

Dylan laughed. 'Alfonse sounds awesome.'

Mr Leonard smiled at Dylan. 'Am I right in thinking we have a sports fan here?'

'How *very* interesting,' said Mr Leonard, flashing a gold tooth.

MEANWHILE, Tom and Carolyn were
watching over Alfonse.
They checked his pulse.
Tested his reflexes.

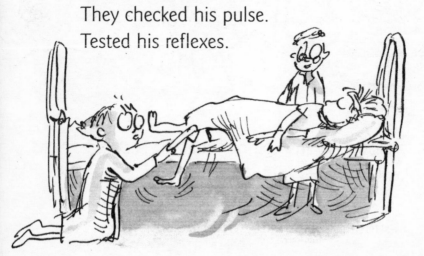

Measured his blood pressure.

Suddenly Alfonse stirred.

'The others?' Alfonse demanded.

'There are only two of us,' said Carolyn.

'But I see eight!' said Alfonse.

Carolyn looked around. 'Nope,' she said. 'Only two!'

'Where am I?'

'You're at **MONSTER HOSPITAL**,' said Carolyn.

'You have a head injury,' said Tom.

'I don't understand,' he said.

'You got hurt in your last football game,' Tom explained.

Alfonse covered his ears. 'Stop it. Why are you all talking at once? Why is everything so **BLURRY?**'

Tom held up one finger. 'How many do you see?'

'Two.'

'Ah, I see,' said Tom.

'What is it?' asked Carolyn.

'**DOUBLE VISION**,' said Tom. 'A common side-effect of head injuries.'

Tom used the Mobile Monster Slit Lamp to look into Alfonse's eye.

Carolyn squirted some fluorescent green drops into it and Tom checked again.

The two doctors tested the elf's vision using an eye chart.

'Read the letters you see.'

'MM, OO, NN, SS, TT, EE, RR ...'

'20/20,' said Tom. 'Except in double. You've damaged the muscles around the orbit.'

'What's the orbit?' asked Carolyn.

'The eye socket.'

'We had better tell your father that you have woken up,' said Carolyn.

'My father?' said Alfonse. 'Is he really here?'

'He flew you here in his helicopter!'
said Tom.

The elf slumped back. 'That's not my dad,'
he said. 'That's Mr Leonard, my manager.
My dad has no idea where I am.'

'What about your mother?'

'She died,' said Alfonse.
Tom and Carolyn
were shocked.

'Exactly where are you from, Alfonse?'
'Exactly where are you from, Alfonse?'
'Can we help you find your dad, Alfonse?'
'Can we help you find your dad, Alfonse?'
There are only so many questions a
one-eyed orphan elf can be asked before he
sits up and ...

'Would you stop *calling* me that?

My name is *not* Alfonse! It's **Alfred**.'
Tom and Carolyn stared.
They were all ears.

Alfred sulked for a while and then spoke.

I wanted to be a famous footballer.

But Mum and Dad thought I was too young. I never joined a team.

Then Mum got sick and died.

Dad made me quit football and help him with his job delivering the post.

47

I hated it so I ran away.
But when I got to the city, the
Monster Catchers caught me ...

... and took me to the
orphanage.

I told them I had no family and
that my name was Alfonse.

Turned out for the best, because
the orphanage had a football team
Orphans United.

They said I was good.

No, they said I was really good.

Actually, they said I was the star.

When I played, the team didn't lose.

Soon Orphans United were winning in the league tables.

Mr Leonard became the manager.

Then he adopted me and took me to live in his mansion.

'And the orphanage just *let* him take you?'
said Tom.

'Yes,' said Alfred. 'Because I lied.

I lied about my name.

I lied about my family.

I lied about my village.

I lied about EVERYTHING cuz I

wanted to be a football star.'

'Don't you miss your family?' asked Carolyn.

Yes! I want my daddy!

There was the sound of approaching footsteps.

Mr Leonard, Sylvie and Dylan burst into the room.

'Did I hear my superstar? You're awake!'

'Is Alfonse making sense?' said Sylvie.

'Perfect sense,' said Carolyn.

'How you doin', buddy?' asked Mr Leonard.

'Two Mr Leonards?' said Alfred.

'**DOUBLE VISION**,' explained Tom.

'Why not?' said Mr Leonard. 'Two of me is better than one!'

'My head hurts,' said Alfred.

'Yes, but you're awake!' said Mr Leonard. 'Awake is good. Awake is excellent!

Awake WINS GAMES!'

'But my head ...'

Mr Leonard stared into Alfred's eye.
Alfred went quiet.
'See? Nothing wrong with YOU, my son!'
'Actually ...' said Carolyn.

'Please come with me and sign this, doctors,' interrupted Mr Leonard.

Tom stayed with Alfred.

RELEASE FORM

This letter is proof that
the footballer

_____ [name]

is **healthy and fit** to compete
in the monster football
championships on May 1st.

_____ [name of doctor]

_____ [name of hospital]

Carolyn had so much to say that she did not know where to begin.

Sylvie spoke first. '**We *are NOT* signing**. He isn't ready to return to football.'

Mr Leonard stamped his foot. 'Don't be ridiculous. Players get hurt. They get back up on their feet. They play again.'

'They get hurt again!' said Carolyn.

'That's crazy,' said Sylvie.
'That's sport,' said Dylan.
'Whose side are **you** on?' snapped Sylvie.
'Mine!' said Mr Leonard.

'This boy understands football,' said
Mr Leonard. 'Yes, this boy is very smart! I bet
you'd like a helicopter ride. And an evening
in my mansion where we have a
Mr Whippy machine ...'

Dylan's eyes shone.
**'I LOVE soft
ice cream.'**

'He's bribing you, Dylan,' said Sylvie.
Mr Leonard cleared his throat. 'In the
morning, we go to the game. Alfonse plays.
You get VIP treatment. ALL-YOU-
CAN-EAT popcorn and
fizzy drinks.'
Dylan was
hopping up
and down.

Mr Leonard handed Dylan his pen. 'You only have to sign here!'

'No, no, don't!' said Sylvie and Carolyn.

'**How could you!**' said Carolyn.
Dylan looked down. 'Sorry, but ...'

'Don't be sorry,' said Mr Leonard. 'Now let's get my son Alfonse and we'll be off!'

'You are not his father!' Carolyn spluttered, running after him. 'And his name is NOT Alfonse. It's ALFRED!'

'What?' asked Sylvie.

'He's a runaway,' said Carolyn. 'His father is alive. We have to help Alfred find his family!'

'What a lot of TROLLSWALLOP!' said Mr Leonard.

Mr Leonard marched into Alfred's room
and scooped him out of bed.

'Alfred can't go,' cried Carolyn.

'His name is ALFONSE!' said Mr Leonard.
'And he's going!'

'He needs medical supervision,' said Tom.

'He'll get it,' said Dylan. 'I'm going with him.'

'What are you talking about?' said Tom.

'STOP IT,' groaned Alfred, covering his eye.

'See?' said Mr Leonard. 'You're upsetting Alfonse. There are too many of you crowding around him.'

'But only one of me,' said Dylan, opening the door.

'You will love the Mr Whippy machine!' said Mr Leonard, trotting ...

... out of the hospital ...

... and into the helicopter.

70

'This is terrible,' said Carolyn.

'I can't believe Mr Leonard just **TOOK** him!' said Tom.

click
click
click

It was Sister Winifred. 'I've never seen such a bunch of glum faces. Can I help?'

'Good,' said Sister Winifred. 'Because look who I found wandering through the castle.'

It was an elf! 'I'm looking for my son, Alfred,' he said.

'Alfred's DAD?' said Tom.

'Do you have proof?' asked Sylvie.

'What a silly question,' said Carolyn. 'They look exactly the same!'

The elf produced a birth certificate. 'See?'
he said. 'Alfred, son of Ulf. That's me.

And if you don't believe that, look at this.'
He opened the newspaper to the sports page.

STAR PLAYER INJURED!

IN THE QUALIFYING GAME FOR THE LEAGUE FINAL,
ORPHANS' STAR PLAYER ALFONSE LEONARD WAS
SERIOUSLY HURT WHEN CAPTAIN FOR
TROLL UNITED SAT ON HIS HEAD. LEONARD
WAS FLOWN TO MONSTER HOSPITAL
BY MANAGER FATHER.

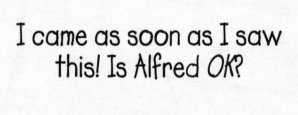

I came as soon as I saw this! Is Alfred *OK?*

'He's going to be fine,' said Tom.
'Head injury,' said Sylvie.
'But he's not here,' said Carolyn.
'**WHAT?**' asked Ulf.

Mr Leonard took Alfred to his mansion. He said he'd adopted him.

Alfred changed his name to Alfonse and said he was an orphan.

He ran away to be a football star!

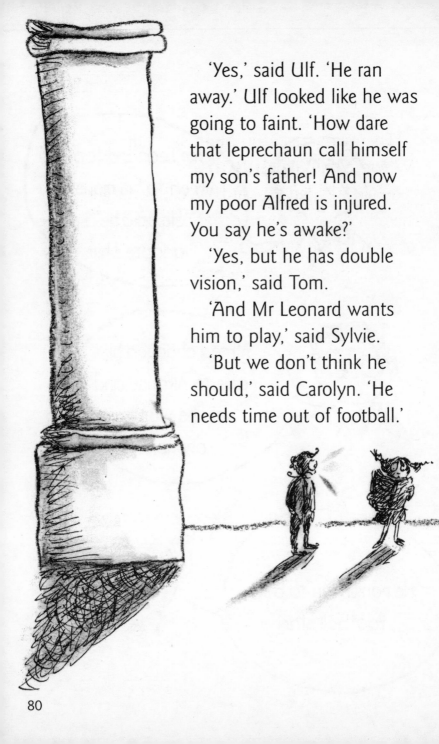

'Yes,' said Ulf. 'He ran away.' Ulf looked like he was going to faint. 'How dare that leprechaun call himself my son's father! And now my poor Alfred is injured. You say he's awake?'

'Yes, but he has double vision,' said Tom.

'And Mr Leonard wants him to play,' said Sylvie.

'But we don't think he should,' said Carolyn. 'He needs time out of football.'

'Then we must stop him!' said Ulf. 'Where is this **mansion?**'

Sylvie stepped forward. 'We'll never get there in time. Our only chance is to go straight to the stadium.'

Carolyn looked at the newspaper. 'But it's miles away!'

click
click
click

Sister Winifred again!
'Now I know that you
children do not like to ask for
help,' she said, looking directly
at Sylvie. 'But you have all
come to the end of a very long
shift at Monster Hospital.
You've done a good job.
While I am a little bit cross
with Dylan, let's
hope he will do
the right thing.
To thank you for
all your hard work,
I want you to
take this.' She handed
them a tube.
ONE-OFF FLYING
OINTMENT.

'Make sure to read the instructions,' Sister Winifred said. 'Use it as you see fit.'

'What does that mean?' asked Carolyn.

'She means we'll figure it out,' said Tom.

Sister Winifred smiled. 'Exactly! Now off you go! No time to waste, doctors! I want you to prove to me that you are the little monsters that I always thought you were ...'

The doctors and the elf hurried out
of the castle ...

... through the **THICK WOOD** ...

... and deep rivers ...

... across stinging beds of **THORNS** and **NETTLES** ...

... to an empty cave where they stopped to rest.

'We'll **NEVER** get there in time,' said
Carolyn, passing sweets around.

Tom looked at his watch. 'You're right.'

'I wish we'd brought more to eat,' said
Carolyn. 'I wish we had a Mr Whippy machine.'

Ulf looked up at the stars. 'I wish I'd listened to my son,' he said. 'When Alfred's mother died, I made him quit football. In a short time, Alfred lost the two things he loved most in the world.' His voice cracked. 'Now I have lost him too!'

'No, Ulf,' said Carolyn. 'I promise you, Alfred wants to come home. He just doesn't know how.'

'But I can't give him a mansion, or rides in a helicopter,' said Ulf.

'None of that matters,' said Tom. 'A son should be with his father.'

'And anyway,' said Sylvie briskly. 'Alfred shouldn't be playing football with a head injury. Or double vision.'

Sylvie looked up at the sun coming up over the Thick Wood. 'We'd better move fast,' she said.

'I can't walk a step farther,' said Carolyn. 'I'm pooped.'

'You're always complaining,' said Tom.

'Have you both forgotten Sister Winifred's present?' said Sylvie, drawing out the ONE-OFF FLYING OINTMENT.

To be used only once, to fly as you fly in your dreams. Suitable for monsters and humans.

'It would speed up the journey,' said Tom.
'Maybe so, but if we all use it now,' said
Carolyn, 'there won't be any left to help
Alfred.'

'True,' said Sylvie, passing the tube to Carolyn. 'But we don't all have to use it at once! Come on. You go first. Rub it on your hands. Let's see what it does.'

Carolyn shook her head.

'I'll go,' said Ulf.

'No,' said Tom. 'You will need the magic when you get to the stadium. If Carolyn won't go, then ...'

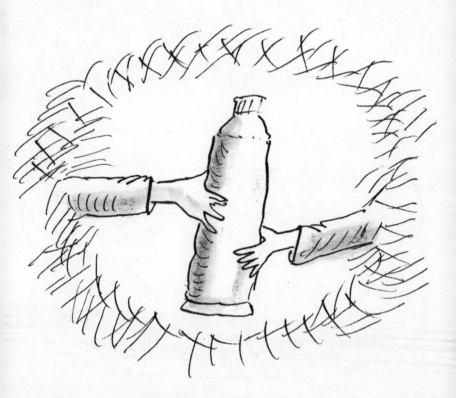

'OK, *fine*,' said Carolyn, squeezing out some cream and rubbing it in.

She looked up at the sky and felt all her worries disappear. She was no longer tired. In fact, she felt light. And strong. She stood on her tippy toes and stretched out her arms. 'Quick, grab on …'

They flew to the stadium.

The game was almost over.
The scoreboard read:

'There's Alfred!' said Ulf, pointing. 'What's he doing?'

Alfred was staring up them. He ran in
a confused circle and toppled over.
The crowd groaned. **TWEET!**
The ref stopped the game.

'ALFRED!' cried Ulf,
running down the steps.
Sylvie, Tom and
Carolyn followed.

Two huge monsters blocked them.

'WHERE DO YOU THINK YOU'RE GOING?'
one said.

'My son has been hurt!' cried Ulf.

'Take a seat!' said the other.

'But I need to help Alfred!'

Suddenly, Dylan appeared,
helping Alfred off the pitch.

Alfred looked up and saw his
father.

In the stadium, a cheer
welled up.

'I've got to get past them,' said
Ulf. Sylvie passed him the
ONE-OFF FLYING OINTMENT.

He squirted some into
his hand and flew down
after Alfred.

103

On the pitch, the players looked confused.
The crowd booed. What was going on?

Then Dylan suddenly ran out onto the pitch. He was wearing Alfred's Number 4 shirt. He took Alfred's position as centre forward. The trolls exchanged worried looks. The whistle blew and the game resumed.

'What's that crazy loon doing?' said Tom.

'Oh oh!' said Sylvie. 'They're giving him a hard time!'

'That must have hurt,' said Tom.

'Maybe they think they have to squash him because he's the sub for the super-star,' said Carolyn.

'Since when are you a
football expert?' said Tom.
'Where is Mr Leonard?'
asked Sylvie. 'He would *never* let Alfred
and Dylan swap places.'

'Maybe Dylan hasn't asked him,' said Tom.

'He's up!' cried Carolyn.

Because the trolls were so busy guarding
Dylan, **ORPHANS UNITED** held on.

With thirty seconds remaining in the game,
the score was still 2-2.

Suddenly Dylan had the ball. He was on a breakaway, running for the goal.

Then the team captain of TROLL CITY stuck out his foot.

Dylan went flying. He landed in a heap.

The whistle blew. The troll was handed a card. But there was no one to help Dylan, for Dylan was the team doctor.

Sylvie reached for the ointment. 'My turn,' she shouted, flying over the monsters and on to the pitch beside Dylan ...

... where she squirted a blob of ONE-OFF FLYING OINTMENT on to the toe of Dylan's football boot. 'I don't know how you are going to do it,' whispered Sylvie, 'but you are going to score.'

Dylan nodded, dazed.

'This is what you've always dreamed about, isn't it? To score the winning goal?'

Dylan stood up.

The ref approached them.

'What's going on?'

Sylvie backed away. 'You were right to sub off Alfred, Dylan,' she yelled. 'You did the right thing – just as Sister Winifred said you would. Look up there!'

In the commotion, Alfred and his father
had snuck out of the dressing room,
flown past Mr Leonard
and now waved down at them.

'I'm going home!'

Alfred shouted.

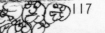

'Penalty kick for *ORPHANS UNITED!*' cried
the ref, pointing at Dylan.

Dylan positioned the ball.

He ran.

He kicked.

He scored!

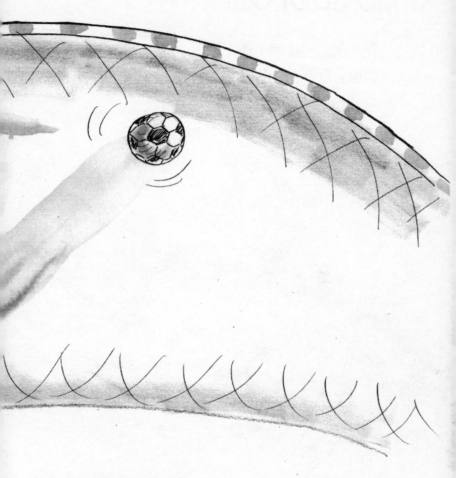

The **ORPHANS UNITED** supporters went wild.
They had won the League Final!
The whistle sounded the end of the game ...
... and the beginning of something else.

For the ball did not stop, as most balls do. Once it had blasted through the net, it kept on going

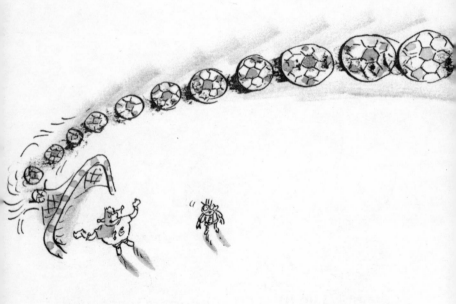

high into the air

to where Tom and Carolyn stood.
They reached up and grabbed on.

It *swooped* to the lower seats
to collect Sylvie

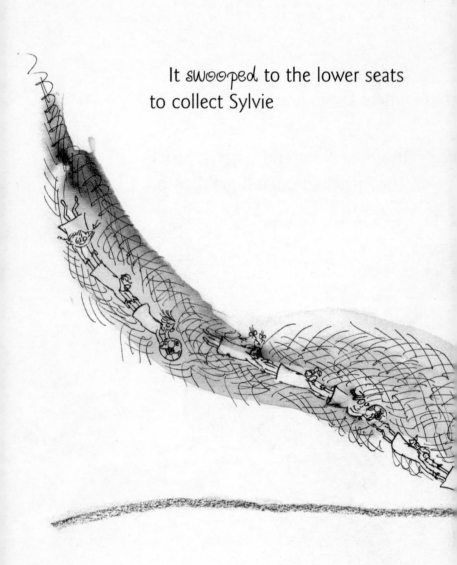

and then down to the pitch
where Dylan grabbed on too.

The ball continued on
its strange journey,
out of the stadium,

higher and higher,

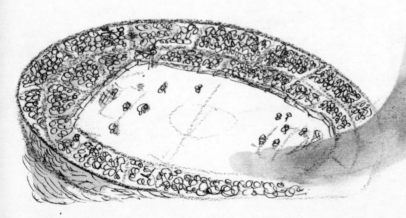

over hills and tree tops ...

... and finally through the window ...

... which was not really a window at all but rather the medicine cabinet that Sister Winifred had warned them they must not, under any circumstances, open.

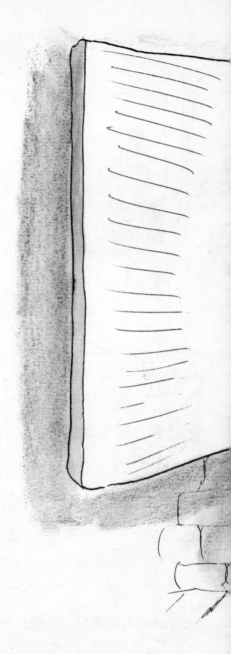

Sylvie, Dylan, Tom and Carolyn looked around.

They were home where their journey had begun not so long ago.

Yes, they had proven they were very much the little monsters that Sister Winifred had hoped.

And they were now good friends too.

And probably late for class ...

Click

click

dick

Hodder
Children's
Books

Turn the page

for more fantastic fiction

from Hodder Children's Books ...

Stone Goblins

Tree Goblin

Puddle Goblin

GOBLINS

By David Melling

Shadow Goblin

Ghost Goblin

CLAUDE

Claude is no ordinary dog – he's the coolest canine on the block! With his faithful sidekick Sir Bobblysock, he leads an extraordinary life of the greatest adventures!

'A wonderful creation for newly independent readers.'
– The Bookseller

www.hodderchildrens.co.uk